D0578724

GROUNDHOG'S HORSE

Joyce Rockwood

GROUNDHOG'S HORSE

drawings by Victor Kalin

Holt, Rinehart and Winston · New York

The story of the giant black racer snake is adapted from a Cherokee tale told to anthropologist James Mooney and recorded by him in "Myths of the Cherokee," *Nineteenth Annual Report of the Bureau of American Ethnology*, Washington, D. C., 1900.

Text copyright © 1978 by Joyce Rockwood Hudson
Illustrations copyright © 1978 by Victor Kalin
All rights reserved, including the right to reproduce this book or portions thereof in any form. Published simultaneously in Canada by Holt, Rinehart and Winston of Canada, Limited.
Printed in the United States of America

10 9 8 7 6 5 4 3

Library of Congress Cataloging in Publication Data

Rockwood, Joyce.
Groundhog's horse.

SUMMARY: An eleven-year-old Cherokee sets off on a one-boy raid of a Creek town to rescue his "unusual" horse.
1. Cherokee Indians—Fiction. 2. Indians of North America—Fiction. 3. Horses—Fiction.
I. Kalin, Victor. II. Title.
PZ7.R597Gr   [Fic]   77–22676
ISBN 0–03–021526–9

ISBN 0-03-021526

This story is for Leah Mayhew

CONTENTS

TO THE READER

The horse in this story is an Indian horse, but that does not mean that she lives out West on the treeless plains or in the dry canyons. Her home is in the South, where magnolia trees bloom and the country is green and warm. The Indian who owns her is a native southerner, a Cherokee. Like the western Indians, the southern Indians owned and loved horses.

The time is 1750, more than twenty years before the American Revolution. British colonists are living along the seaboard of Georgia and the Carolinas, but most of the South is still a land of Indians. The Cherokees are mountain people. Their towns are in the narrow valleys of the Appalachian Mountains in northern Georgia, western North Carolina, and eastern Tennessee. South of the Cherokees are the Creek Indians, their towns and villages scattered from the rolling hills of northern Georgia and Alabama down into Florida. The Creeks and Cherokees in this year 1750 are enemies, as they have been for many years, their warriors making constant raids against each other's towns. . . .

J.R.

THE RACE

Groundhog had just finished making the forelock of his small black mare a thing of beauty, plaiting it with a string of costly beads, red and white. "How do you like it?" he asked as he stopped before Grandfather to show it off.

Grandfather was sitting in the shade, leaning back against the earth-plastered wall of their house. At Groundhog's voice he raised his head and opened his eyes, blinking sleepily. "What did you say?" he grumbled.

Too late Groundhog realized his mistake. "Were you sleeping?" he asked.

Grandfather rubbed at the rheumatism in his back and glared at his grandson. "No," he said irritably. "I was dancing. I had my left foot tied to my right elbow and there was a turkey perched on my head."

Groundhog sighed. It was always like this between Grandfather and him.

"I'm sorry I woke you," he said.

"So am I," grumbled Grandfather. "I was having a very pleasant nap."

Groundhog gave a little tug at the rope tied about his horse's neck. She was searching the bare ground for a stray blade of grass. "Come on, Midnight," he said, and she raised her head at her name.

"What is *that?*" demanded Grandfather, pointing to her forelock.

"It is what I came to show you," said Groundhog.

"Beads on a horse?" snorted Grandfather. "That is the most ridiculous thing I have seen all day."

Groundhog sighed and dug with his big toe at a pebble half buried in the ground.

"When are you going to quit this childish thing with your horse?" said Grandfather. "You are eleven years old, almost a warrior. It is time to act like it."

Almost a warrior? Groundhog looked down at himself. He was growing, but he was not yet as tall as a man. And he was skinny, so skinny that keeping up the belt of his breechcloth required a constant effort.

"All the town laughs about you and your horse," Grandfather said. "And why shouldn't they? It is what you deserve for going around telling people how unusual she is. 'Is she a fast runner?' they ask. 'No,' you say. 'Just unusual.'"

Groundhog shifted uncomfortably. He had never been able to make anyone understand about Midnight.

"How unusual can a horse be?" said Grandfather. "You tell people she has courage and intelligence and a

4

strong heart with all the best qualities. What kind of talk is that? Horses don't have courage and intelligence. They have flies and foamy sweat. They are four-legged animals. Burden bearers. It is your imagination that makes more of her. It is your own foolishness that makes you think she would like beads plaited into her forelock. People laugh at you."

Groundhog had worked the pebble loose with his big toe and now he flipped it out of its hole and watched with satisfaction as it bounced with a tiny clink off a piece of broken pottery.

Grandfather sighed. He rubbed at his rheumatism and leaned back against the wall to continue his nap. "A boy should listen to his grandfather," he said as he closed his eyes. "I am trying to tell you that horse of yours is just a horse. That is all she is."

Groundhog knew better than to say more. He glanced at Midnight and she met his eyes with a look that assured him she was not a product of his foolish imagination. He reached out and stroked her, feeling the lovely smoothness of her neck. But his spirits were low as he led her away.

Groundhog wandered among the bark-roofed houses of Frogtown. The houses—some standing in clusters, some alone—were scattered around a big open space used for dances and games and council meetings. Frogtown was not a large town, but it was full of life—full of people and dogs and horses; cats, chickens, and crying babies. Overhead a haze of wood smoke, light and misty, moved softly with the summer breezes. It came from all the cookfires in the bare dirt yards and it gave a comfortable feeling to the air.

But Groundhog was not paying attention to cheery things. Grandfather had ruined his good mood. The beaded forelock was not such a ridiculous thing. Other people tied ribbons and feathers in their horses' manes. Beads might be more valuable, but he had made only a short string. And they did look nice against her shiny blackness.

Groundhog glanced around at his neighbors as he passed them in their yards. Most were busy pounding corn or feathering arrows or stirring food as it simmered in brass kettles on the open fires. A few looked up and waved at him. But not a single person pointed to the beaded forelock and fell over laughing, as Grandfather had predicted.

Groundhog's spirits began to rise. Grandfather was not going to ruin such a fine summer day. Not even the bothersome flies and mosquitoes could ruin all the pleasure to be found in this mountain valley, so green and alive with summer.

He stopped for a moment to watch the walls going up on the third log house to be built in Frogtown. The idea of log houses was new. It came from the white people in the British colonies along the seaboard, five days to the east. According to Grandfather, it was also the whites who first brought horses, cats, and chickens, brass kettles, guns, and lots of other things. Groundhog could remember when there were no log houses, only the sturdy Cherokee houses with walls woven of sticks and plastered with clay, and roofs shingled with bark.

For a little while he watched the men work on the new house. Then he decided to look for Jumper and perhaps get a war game going. But first he would have to do something with Midnight. Horses were no good for playing war. They could not walk quietly or cover their trail or climb a tree to hide. So he headed for the outlying pasture where the town herd was grazing. He would leave her there and come back to town to find Jumper.

Groundhog had led Midnight as far as the edge of town when he was stopped by the call of a redbird—Jumper's signal. He looked around and spotted his friend near the cornfield. Little Hawk and Pinecone were with him and all had their horses. Groundhog went over, leading Midnight.

"Fancy horse," said Jumper, nodding at Midnight's forelock.

There was teasing in his tone and Groundhog eyed him suspiciously. All three of his friends looked too cheerful, as if they were up to something.

"Looks like she's dressed up for racing," said Pinecone.

So that was it. They all knew how much he didn't like to race, even though he would never admit it. Midnight, though unusual in many ways, was not out-

7

standing on the raceground. When Groundhog told people Midnight was unusual, they thought he was saying that she was a fast runner. To them there was nothing else about a horse that could be unusual. So when she lost a race, it really tickled them. "What an unusual horse!" they would mock.

He had given up trying to explain his horse to his friends. It would be easier to explain them to Midnight. She had a better understanding of things in her right ear than his friends would have if they pooled theirs all together.

"We can't go to the raceground," he said, trying to work his way out. "Not while we're at war with the Creeks. It's too far to go. There could be a Creek raiding party out there. One minute we would be racing and the next minute dead. Or captured."

"That's not going to happen," said Jumper.

"Sure it's not," said Groundhog. "That's just what Red Turtle thought. He was playing around down there in Creek country without fear of anything when our warriors caught him and brought him back here. One day he was a Creek and the next day an adopted Cherokee. Is that what you want? To be carried down to Creek country and never see your people again?"

"I could escape," said Little Hawk.

Groundhog shook his head. "Has Red Turtle ever escaped? His Cherokee family watches every move he makes. If he even gets a funny look in his eye like he might be thinking of slipping away, they see it. Then they make him sleep close between two people at night. They know every move he makes, every breath he takes."

"This is the dumbest conversation I ever heard," said Jumper. "All we're suggesting is a little race. Everybody that's not a coward, come on."

Groundhog sighed, giving in.

The raceground was downriver, beyond the cornfield, through some woods, and out of sight of the town. It was not safe to go there unless there were warriors along for protection. It was not safe, and it was not allowed.

"Someone will catch us leaving," said Groundhog as they pulled themselves up onto their horses and started out.

"The trick is to act normal," said Jumper. "As long as we don't look guilty, no one will think we're doing anything wrong. They'll think we've been sent on an errand or something."

Jumper led the way down to the Frogtown River. At the water's edge they turned up the path that led past the cornfield and through the woods to the raceground. Groundhog was miserable. With each step they were closer to a race Midnight was sure to lose. And on top of that, he was afraid of the Creeks. They were terrible enemies. He hoped some adult would notice them leaving and call them back. But the woods soon closed in around them.

After a time they arrived at the raceground, a long

stretch of flat open land. On one side was the river. On the other side, dark woods.

Midnight stepped nervously and blew out a fluttery snort. She looked toward the woods, her ears pricked. Groundhog looked where she was looking, half expecting to see a Creek raiding party standing in the forest shadows. But he saw nothing. Perhaps she was only uneasy about the race.

He lined up with the others at the end of the race-ground. His mind now was on the race. He stroked Midnight's neck, wishing he had not let himself get trapped into doing this. She was an unusual horse, but only once had she ever won a race.

Jumper gave the signal. The horses leaped forward, the boys whooping and yelling as they flew down the course. Groundhog leaned close against Midnight's neck, pleading with her to win, urging her frantically, "Let's go, let's go, let's go, let's go!"

Then it happened. Mounted warriors, painted and terrible, burst out of the woods before them, galloping into their path. Groundhog yelled in terror as he reined Midnight in. She reared and plunged. Everything whirled. Then she steadied and Groundhog looked wildly about, searching for an escape.

But as his eyes swept the warriors, his mouth flew open in surprise.

There was Kingfisher, his own older brother. And the others—they were all Cherokees. These warriors with bold tattoos upon their chests and eagle feathers dangling from their hair were all their own older brothers. And in their hands were long, limber switches.

Groundhog braced himself as the warriors began to scold. Suddenly the air was singing with the whir of their switches.

"Are you boys crazy?" fussed the older brothers. "What do you mean coming out here alone? Do you want to get captured by Creeks and make your mothers cry?"

The switches whirred through the air, snapping against bare skin.

The stinging blows fell on Groundhog's shoulders, on his chest, his arms, his back. "That's enough!" he cried, trying to bat the switches away.

The warriors laughed and laid on a few more blows before throwing down the switches.

"Now you boys look pretty," said Jumper's older brother grinning at them.

Groundhog looked down at the red stripes on his chest and arms. This was the worst part of being switched: not the little bit of pain, but the striped welts that showed to all the world that a boy had been caught doing wrong. The people back in Frogtown would laugh to see the stripes. Laughter was the worst punishment of all.

As they started back toward home, Groundhog moved over to ride beside Kingfisher. "Couldn't we wait until dark to go home?" Groundhog quietly asked his brother. "Then not so many people would see us."

Kingfisher seemed to feel a little sorry for him, but he shook his head. "If you wanted not to be shamed," he said, "you should have stayed near the town."

"Lucky for you we weren't that Creek war party," said Jumper's older brother.

"*What* Creek war party?" Groundhog asked in alarm.

"The one Yellow Dog spotted up the river a little while ago," said Kingfisher.

"When they heard, all the mothers started counting children," said Jumper's older brother. "You four were missing, so they sent us out to look for you. They were afraid you had been captured."

"How did you find us?" asked Jumper.

The warriors laughed.

"You boys were as easy to follow as snakes through the sand," said Kingfisher.

The warriors laughed harder, slapping their thighs.

Groundhog was not amused.

Things got even worse when they neared the town. A shout went up when they were spotted, and everyone quit what they were doing and came to stand at the edge of town, waiting for them.

"Go home, people," Groundhog muttered under his breath. "Don't you have better things to do?"

"Maybe they do," said Jumper. "Let's take a long time at putting our horses in the pasture. Maybe everyone will get tired of waiting for us and go back to their work."

Jumper's older brother overheard. "Here, boys,

we'll take your horses for you so you can greet your friends," he said, teasing them.

"Thanks," Groundhog said sourly.

The four boys climbed down from their horses, and the warriors rode away and left them standing alone, facing the dreadful throng of friends and relatives.

Groundhog looked down at the welts on his skin, feeling embarrassed.

"I'm sorry I got us into this," said Jumper.

"I'm sorry you did, too," said Pinecone.

"It was my fault," said Jumper. "I'll go first. I'll take the brunt of it." He set out ahead of the others.

But Groundhog could not let his friend go alone, not with all those people laughing and hooting at him. No matter whose fault it was, they were comrades and they should all go together. He ran to catch up and Little Hawk and Pinecone followed. Together the four of them walked into town, looking straight ahead, pretending that nothing unusual had happened.

People kept serious faces as they approached. But as soon as they passed by, the laughter started. Groundhog flinched as someone commented loudly on their pretty new shirts with the nice red stripes. Then someone said something about red stripes of war paint. Someone else shouted a mock war whoop. Soon everyone was laughing.

Groundhog hurried to his house and sulked about inside for the rest of the day. His mother and grandfather left him alone. But Pokeberry, his older sister, felt sorry for him and gave him a bowl of cornmush and blackberries to make him feel better.

It was not until the sun was going down that Groundhog suddenly remembered the Creek war party. Maybe they had come to steal horses in the night. "Midnight!" he said, jumping to his feet and hurrying out of the house.

"That horse again," grumbled Grandfather. "What is he going to do now?"

Groundhog went out behind the town to the place where the horses were grazing. A guard was already posted there, and Kingfisher was to take the post later and guard the horses until dawn. But for Groundhog that was not enough. He found Midnight and led her back into the town and tied her outside his house.

"There," he told her. "Now you'll be safe. The Creeks might steal every horse out there, but they won't get you."

Midnight nudged her head against him.

"And listen, girl," he said softly. "I know that you were losing that race. But don't worry about it. Races don't prove anything. Very ordinary horses win races."

He stroked her nose and looked at her. "But it would help if you could run a little faster," he said. "It's embarrassing for me when you lose. You won a race once, do you remember? Maybe you should think about that and try to remember how you did it."

Midnight blinked sleepily, and Groundhog turned and went into the house.

"Are you going to leave that horse there?" grumbled Grandfather. "Right by the door?"

Groundhog almost snapped back at him. "Yes, I am," he said. "Right by the door. I don't want her stolen tonight."

Groundhog's mother shot him a disapproving look for talking so sharply. He sighed and went over and flopped down on his bed. He had had an awful day.

RAID!

When Groundhog woke up with the first light of dawn, his first thought was of Midnight. But it had been a quiet night, with no cries of alarm. The Creek raiding party must have been headed for some other town.

He got up, yawning and stretching, and stumbled sleepily through the dark house. The others of his family were just waking up. He pushed aside the mat hanging in the doorway and stepped out into the dim grayness of the early morning.

He turned to greet Midnight, reaching out his hand to pet her. Then for a moment he stood confused, staring in bewilderment at the empty spot where she was supposed to be. He ran and looked around the corner of the house. And then around the other corner.

"She's gone!" he cried. "Raid! Raid! My horse is gone! Raid!"

Warriors came tumbling out of their houses carrying tomahawks and bows and slinging quivers of ar-

17

rows across their backs. A few had guns they had gotten from the British traders.

"Where? they cried. "Which way did they go?""

"I don't know!" wailed Groundhog. "My horse is gone! They stole Midnight! Those rotten Creeks! They stole my horse!"

Kingfisher came running from his guard post. "What is it?" he cried. "What's going on?"

"Your brother here says his horse was stolen," said one of the warriors. They were all standing around now, looking doubtful.

"I didn't see a raiding party," said Kingfisher. "All the other horses are all right. Maybe Midnight just wandered away."

"She couldn't have," said Groundhog. "I tied her myself. It was a good knot."

Now the warriors looked at each other, rolling their eyes in amusement. "Don't forget," said one of them. "She *is* an unusual horse. Perhaps she untied the knot herself."

They all burst out laughing.

Groundhog looked at Kingfisher. "My older brother," he pleaded softly, "the Creeks stole my horse. I know they did."

Kingfisher was not laughing with the others. But even so, he did not believe Midnight had been stolen. "She is the only horse that is gone," Kingfisher explained. "Why would the Creeks come all the way into the middle of town to steal one horse? She must have gotten loose, that's all. I'll go look for her as soon as the sun is up. I doubt she's wandered far."

"She was *stolen*," said Groundhog. "You warriors are supposed to go after stolen horses. Are you going to let the Creeks make fools of you?"

But the warriors were not listening to him. They went back to their houses for breakfast.

Groundhog sat down miserably by his house and quietly called them unmentionable names.

The light of dawn crept slowly through the town.

A redbird whistled.

Groundhog looked up and saw Jumper.

"She's gone," said Groundhog.

"I heard," said Jumper.

"The Creeks stole her."

"That's not what they are saying," said Jumper.

"That's because they are crazy. They are crazy, and cowards, and fools, and—"

"Hey!" said Jumper. "What's this?" He reached over Groundhog's head and took a small wooden tablet from a crack in the wall.

Groundhog got up to look at it.

"Kingfisher!" he shouted. "Kingfisher! Come look!"

His brother stuck his head outside. He had been guarding horses half the night, and he was tired. "What now?" he asked wearily.

"Come look at this," said Groundhog. "A message for you. And for all the warriors. It's from the Creeks. It was stuck in the wall of our house."

Kingfisher came out to look at it, the rest of the family following behind him. "Did you put it there?" Kingfisher asked suspiciously.

"No, I didn't," said Groundhog. "How could I have made it? Look, I don't even have a knife with me."

Kingfisher looked at him, and then at Jumper, who opened his hands and turned around to show he had no knife either.

"The Creeks put it there," said Groundhog. "They put it there when they stole Midnight. Look what it says. They are telling us about their raid. They are laughing at us."

"What does it say?" asked Grandfather, sounding almost cheerful.

But Kingfisher was upset. He had been a guard when the Creeks had sneaked into the town. They had made a fool of him.

He took the tablet from Jumper. "First there's a picture of a horse," he said irritably.

"That's Midnight," said Groundhog.

"And then a picture of people sleeping," said Kingfisher.

"Look," said Groundhog, pointing to the tablet. "They even drew a dog sleeping."

Grandfather laughed. "Not even the dogs woke up."

Kingfisher ignored their comments. "Next," he said, "they drew a picture of themselves leading the horse away. There are two warriors, you see. And they are Creeks—you can tell by the hair."

"What's this last picture?" asked Groundhog.

"It looks like a rabbit," said Kingfisher.

"Rabbit-town," said Grandfather. "The war party came from Rabbit-town."

"Where's that?" said Groundhog.

"It's downriver in low hill country," said Grandfather. "The Rabbit-town Creeks have been fighting back and forth with the Overhill Cherokees for years. But they've never stopped here to bother us. They've always gone around us. We're lucky it was only a horse they took from us. They steal children from the Overhills."

"Well," Groundhog said to his brother, "are you going to get my horse back?"

"I guess so," grumbled Kingfisher. "You should have left her out with the other horses. Then you would still have her. It would have saved us all a lot of trouble."

Groundhog shrugged. It was true, but he was not going to admit it. How could he have known that the Rabbit-town Creeks were going to be showing off with a stunt like this?

Kingfisher ambled away to summon the warriors.

"I don't think he's very excited about it," said Grandfather as the family went back into the house.

"I don't care if he's not excited," said Groundhog. "Just so he rescues my horse."

"For one horse I don't think anybody will be excited," said Grandfather.

21

In a little while Kingfisher returned. "They won't go," he said, sitting down calmly at the fire to eat his breakfast.

"They won't go?" exclaimed Groundhog.

Kingfisher looked up at the ceiling, cocking his head. "There seems to be an echo in here," he said.

"They won't *go?*" Groundhog spluttered again.

"A double echo," said Kingfisher.

"Why *won't* they go?" demanded Groundhog.

"Too much work," said Kingfisher.

"Are you joking?" said Groundhog.

"No," said Kingfisher.

"I think he means too much work for only one horse," said Grandfather. "It is not as if the Creeks killed somebody last night, or captured a child, or stole a whole herd of horses. One horse was all they took."

"But it was Midnight. And it would be easy to get her back," argued Groundhog. "There's nothing to it. Just go down to Rabbit-town, sneak in at night like they did, and steal her back again. You don't have to do any fighting. Just sneak in and steal her."

"No fighting?" said Kingfisher. "What if somebody wakes up?"

"*We* didn't wake up," said Groundhog. "They came all the way into the middle of town. They came right to our door. And nobody heard them at all."

"Well, if it's so terribly easy to steal a horse, why don't you go do it yourself?" said Kingfisher.

"Because I'm not a warrior," said Groundhog.

22

"He certainly is not," said Groundhog's mother. "He's just a boy."

"I didn't really mean that he should do it," said Kingfisher.

"But you meant what you said about not going after Midnight," said Groundhog.

"I can't help it, little brother," said Kingfisher. "I tried to get up a war party, but no one wanted to be bothered. I'm sorry."

Groundhog turned angrily and left the house. Jumper was waiting outside for him. Without speaking they headed down to the river and climbed up into the tree that the two of them used for their councils.

"They're not going after her," Groundhog said grimly as he settled onto his limb.

"I know," said Jumper. "I was listening."

"What do you think I should do?" asked Groundhog.

"Get another horse," said Jumper.

Groundhog gave him a pained look.

"What else can you do?" said Jumper.

"Go after her myself," said Groundhog.

"Wait now," said Jumper. "Kingfisher didn't mean that you should really do it. You're not a warrior."

"The only reason I'm not a warrior is that I'm not old enough to be one. But I can do everything a warrior can do. Like going through the woods without leaving a trail. Can you ever find me when I hide?"

"Not usually," admitted Jumper.

"Can you hear me when I sneak up on you?"

"Not always," said Jumper.

"Can anyone our age run as fast as I can?"

"No," said Jumper. "But it's only because your legs are longer. There's no need to get carried away with yourself."

"I'm not getting carried away," said Groundhog. "I'm simply pointing out that I can do what needs to be done."

"Can you hit somebody in the head with a toma-hawk?"

"That's not what needs to be done," said Ground-hog.

"How do you know?" said Jumper. "What if they catch you?"

"They won't," said Groundhog. "No one will wake up. I know how to move quietly. There won't be any danger."

"No danger? Just yesterday you thought horseracing was dangerous."

"That was before Midnight was stolen," said Groundhog. "Everything is different now."

"Well then," said Jumper, hesitating, "do you want me to come with you?"

"Would you like to?" asked Groundhog.

"Not too much," said Jumper. "It's not that I'm afraid. But . . . well, you see, my moccasins are getting thin. I don't think they would hold up on a long trip."

Groundhog thought it a poor excuse but did not say so.

"How far is it to Rabbit-town?" Jumper then asked.

"I don't know," said Groundhog. "A day's journey. Maybe two."

"No, I think it's farther than that," said Jumper. "A lot farther."

Groundhog shrugged. "I'll take a good supply of cold meal. I won't starve."

"Do you really think your grandfather will let you go?" said Jumper.

"Of course not," said Groundhog. "I'm going to have to sneak away. Tonight. After everyone has gone to sleep."

"Too bad," said Jumper. "I wanted to watch you whoop out of town like a warrior. With everybody cheering and singing."

"That would have been nice," Groundhog agreed. "That lazy bunch of warriors could go whooping out of town if they wanted. But when a boy goes on the war trail, he has to sneak away like a weasel."

LEAVING TOWN

Groundhog made his plans. His first problem was to decide what to take. He would need a good supply of cold meal. It was the perfect food for traveling. Just a spoonful or two of the parched cornmeal in a bowl of water would swell up to make a bowlful of mush. With cold meal he would not have to waste time hunting or fishing along the way.

The other thing he needed was an extra pair of moccasins in case his present pair wore out; he had an extra pair in a basket beneath his bed.

But getting the things together was the real problem. He lived in a house full of people. How could he fill a sack with cold meal and pull out his extra moccasins without someone asking what he was doing? Getting cold meal was going to be the toughest. It was kept near the hearth in the middle of their one-room house, out where everybody could see.

Groundhog hung around home all afternoon waiting for a chance at the cold meal. But never once was he left entirely alone. The cold meal stayed in its large clay jar. The deerskin pouch he was planning to fill stayed flat and empty.

By the time night fell, Groundhog was worried. Everyone was gathered around the fire inside the house. Groundhog's sister, his brother, his mother, and his grandfather all sat contentedly and watched the low flames flit across the coals in the hearth. Groundhog sat miserably and eyed the nearby jar of cold meal. Without it, he could not make the journey.

After a while, Kingfisher began to nod sleepily. He had stayed up all the night before guarding horses, and even though it was early in the evening, his eyes drooped and his head nodded. He gave a little snore. Then, with an effort, he opened his eyes halfway. "I'm going to bed," he mumbled sleepily. "I've had a hard day."

Not as hard as it should have been, thought Groundhog, feeling his brother should have been out on the war trail rescuing Midnight.

But as he watched Kingfisher crawl into bed, Groundhog had an idea. He waited and when at last he heard him snoring, he said to the others at the fire, "Do you think he might go out tomorrow to bring Midnight back?"

"I don't think so, my son," said his mother. "Nothing will be different tomorrow."

"Well," Groundhog said innocently, "I think I'll fix a bag of cold meal for him, just in case he wakes up early and wants to go."

Grandfather shook his head. "That's foolish," he muttered.

"It's just in case," said Groundhog. "You never know when Kingfisher might change his mind about something. Tomorrow he won't be so tired as he was today. If he wakes up in the morning and decides to go after Midnight, I want things to be all ready for him."

He took the deerskin pouch and filled it with cold meal, then pushed a little gourd bowl down into the meal and drew the pouch shut. He set it near the door. "Just in case he needs it," he said again. Then he sat down on his own bed.

When he was sure no one was looking, he leaned down and reached beneath the bed, groped through a basket, and pulled out his extra pair of moccasins. He stuck them back out of sight underneath his bed, near his regular pair, in a place where he could easily find them in the dark. Then he felt to make sure his knife was on his belt. Everything was set. Now all that remained for him to do was wait for everyone to go to sleep.

Except for Kingfisher, everyone stayed up unusually late that night. The jokes and stories around the fire seemed to go on forever. Sometimes there would be a lull when no one said anything and all sat quietly and watched the flames. Then Groundhog would fake a yawn that would set everyone to yawning. But no one made a move to go to bed.

Grandfather was growing more friendly and talkative as the fire warmed his rheumatism. He smiled at Groundhog's yawning. "Are my stories boring you?" he asked. "Perhaps I should tell you about the hunter and the black racer snake."

Groundhog did not want another story. But he tried to look interested.

"By black racer," said Grandfather, "I do not mean an ordinary snake. I mean a black racer this big around," and he held his hands to show a circle as big as a man's head. "I mean a black racer so long it can coil itself around this house. So fast that nothing lives that can escape its pursuit. Certainly no man can run faster."

Groundhog perked up in spite of himself and began listening.

"This great snake has its home in the high mountains," said Grandfather.

"In the dismal places?" asked Groundhog.

"Yes," said Grandfather. "It is like other monsters. You will not find it in the valleys where people live. It stays high up the slopes, up where wild rivers tumble down rocky gaps, where sunlight moves dimly through deep forests on steep mountain faces. This black racer I am telling you about lives near a certain large up-rooted tree on a particular mountain near Logtown. It keeps constant watch, and whenever it can spring upon an unsuspecting hunter, it coils about him and crushes out his life in its folds. Then it drags the dead body down the mountainside into a deep hole in the river below.

"Now, a man went once to visit some relatives in

Logtown, which is in a valley south of that mountain where the black racer lives. The man was a great hunter, and after resting in his relatives' house a day or two, he got ready to go hunting in the mountains. His friends warned him not to go north, telling him of the danger of the great black racer. The man listened quietly to the warning, but their words only excited his curiosity. He wanted to see this monster for himself.

"Without letting his friends know what he meant to do, he left the town and, as soon as he was out of sight, turned and went directly up the ridge toward the north. All morning he walked, making his way into the high mountains until he was deep in the dismal places, far from any human settlement. His friends had told him where the snake lived, and without any trouble he found the fallen tree. He climbed upon the trunk, and there, sure enough, stretched out in the grass on the other side was the great black racer. Its head was raised but it was looking the other way.

"The huge snake was such a fearsome sight that the hunter was frightened and jumped down and started to run. Hearing the noise, the snake turned quickly and came after him.

"Up the ridge the hunter ran, the snake close behind him, then down the other side toward the river. Though the hunter was running with all his might, the snake gained rapidly. Just as the hunter reached the low ground near the river, the snake caught up with him and wrapped around him, pinning one arm down by his side, but leaving the other one free.

"The snake gave him a terrible squeeze that almost

31

broke his ribs, and then it began to drag him along toward the water. With his free hand the hunter clutched frantically at a bush, but the snake turned its great black head and blew its sickening breath into his face until he had to let go his hold. Again and again the same thing happened as the man clutched at every bush they passed. And all the while they were getting nearer to a deep hole in the river.

"Then, almost at the last moment, a lucky thought came into the hunter's mind. He suddenly remembered having heard that snakes cannot stand the smell of perspiration. He was sweating all over, so he worked his free hand around under his armpit until it was covered with perspiration. Then, drawing it out, he grasped at a bush. As before, the snake turned its head, but this time the hunter slapped his sweaty hand on its nose. The great snake gave a gasp as if it had been wounded. It loosened its coil and glided swiftly away through the bushes.

"The hunter lay panting and then slowly lifted himself to his feet. He was bruised but glad to be alive, and as quickly as he could, he made his way down from the dismal places. When at last he reached Logtown, his relatives greeted him joyfully, for they had guessed where he had gone and had feared he would never return."

Groundhog let out a long, shivering breath. "I wouldn't have ever gone up there alone," he said.

"People do foolish things," said Grandfather and stood up and yawned and stretched. Pokeberry got up.

And so did Groundhog's mother. They were going to bed at last.

"I'll get the fire," said Groundhog.

He waited until they had all reached their beds and then used a piece of broken pottery to scoop ashes over the flickering coals. He made his way to his bed in darkness. No one could see that he still wore his knife as he crawled beneath his blanket. For a long time he lay waiting for the others to fall asleep, until, without intending to, he fell asleep himself.

Suddenly he awoke with a start. Was it too late? Was it morning?

He looked up through the smokehole in the roof. When he saw stars, he knew it was still night.

Groundhog listened to make sure everyone was asleep. Then, very quietly, he sat up and swung his feet down to the floor. He sat still and listened. No one stirred. Very carefully he reached down under his bed, pulled out his two pairs of moccasins, and fastened them to his belt.

As he stood up, his heart began to pound. He picked his way slowly through the dark. When he came to the place where he thought he had put the pouch of cold meal, he stooped and felt for it. It wasn't there. He moved his hands out across the floor, trying to find it. It was gone!

He took a step forward, still stooping, and frantically swept his hands across the floor. As one hand found the cold meal, the other thunked against a pottery jar filled with water.

Groundhog froze, holding his breath, listening. Someone turned over in bed, but that was all. The house was silent again. Picking up the cold meal, Groundhog straightened up very slowly and tiptoed outside into the moonlight.

All was still and quiet. Groundhog looked about nervously. He wanted to let go and run. But that was not the way, not unless he wanted to be caught before he had even started. So he stood still instead and tried to think about what he was doing.

Dogs were what worried him most. Even if he were creeping as quietly as possible, they might hear him. And guards would be a problem, too. He wondered how those Creeks had managed to slip in and out of town the night before.

Of one thing he was certain. The Creeks had come in quietly. He took a long look around and then started out, slowly, carefully, silently—creeping toward the edge of town.

Suddenly a dog barked, and several others took it up. Groundhog pressed himself close against the side of a house and stood without moving for a long time. After things grew quiet, he went on. The dogs did not bark again.

The next problem came when he reached the edge of town. There was an open space between the last house in town and the field of tall corn that stretched down to the river. If he could reach the corn, it would give him cover to the river. But guards were stationed around the town, and they were supposed to keep an eye on all the open spaces. What if they mistook him for a Creek and shot at him? Groundhog tried not to think about it.

He looked up at the night sky. There was too much moonlight. A few clouds moved slowly, drifting beneath the stars. He would have to wait for one of them to cover the moon and darken things up a bit. So he squatted down and waited, watching the sky and worrying that dawn would arrive before he could get away.

At last a cloud came and moved across the moon and everything was pitch black.

"Here I come, Midnight!" he whispered as he rose and sprinted out across the open space, stooping low, running as lightly, as noiselessly, as he could.

The tasseled cornstalks, cool and dark, closed in around his head and Groundhog ran on, leaving Frogtown behind.

HEADING SOUTH

Coming out of the cornfield, Groundhog turned onto the path that ran south along the river. It was the path to Rabbit-town. That was all he knew. He had no idea how far he would have to go. Birdtown was the last Cherokee town before Creek country. He would have to pass it. But then what? Would Rabbit-town be the first Creek town he came to? Or the second? Or the third? How would he know which town it was? Midnight would be there, Groundhog finally decided. That was how he would know.

The cloud that had covered the moon had been joined by others. It was dark, too dark, with no moonlight on the path. As he trotted along in the darkness, Groundhog began to feel frightened. Who knew what was hiding in the blackness? Bears? Cougars? Creeks? There could be a Creek warrior behind every tree. A huge war party. Maybe they were watching him as he got farther and farther from home. Maybe they were watching him, laughing to themselves because he was moving into their trap.

Groundhog began to run faster, looking from one side to the other, straining to see into the darkness. Suddenly he heard a sound. Glancing back, he thought he saw a man stepping from the shadows.

He gasped and ran harder, as fast as he could.

A dark form stepped into his path. Groundhog dodged, but too late. He crashed into the unmoving chest of a warrior. Strong arms grasped him, and he struggled, kicking and pulling, trying to get away.

"Whoa, now!" said the warrior. Groundhog felt the man's big hands feeling up and down his arms and chest. "What is this?" asked the warrior. "A puny man or just a boy?"

"A boy," gasped Groundhog.

"What did you say?" demanded his captor.

"A boy," repeated Groundhog, his voice squeaking with fright.

"You're speaking Cherokee," said the man.

"So are you," said Groundhog, suddenly realizing it.

The two arms relaxed their hold. In the darkness a face leaned down and peered closely into his.

"I'm a Cherokee like you are," said Groundhog in a rush of relief.

"So it seems," said the warrior. "Sorry to scare you like that. We thought you were a Creek stumbling into our camp."

As Groundhog wondered who *we* were, two other warriors stepped out of the darkness.

"What are you doing out here in the dark of night,

38

little brother?" one of the warriors asked good-naturedly. Groundhog could barely see them, but he could tell by the way they talked that they were Overhill Cherokees, from the other side of the mountains.

"Well . . ." Groundhog said, stalling for time as he tried to invent an answer. He was afraid they would take him home if he told the truth.

"Are you lost?" asked the third warrior.

"Yes," lied Groundhog. "I'm lost."

"How did that happen?"

"Um . . ." said Groundhog.

"Were you traveling with your family?" asked a warrior.

"Yes," said Groundhog. "I was traveling with my family."

"And you got separated?"

"Yes," said Groundhog. "A Creek war party came."

"Did your people get killed?"

"No," said Groundhog, beginning to get tangled in his story. "Just separated. We all ran different ways. The Creeks chased me for a long time, but I finally lost them. I went back to find my family, but they were gone. I guess they went on home."

"Probably thought you'd been captured," said one of the warriors.

"Maybe," said Groundhog.

"You must be from Birdtown," said a warrior. "You're headed in that direction."

"Yes," fibbed Groundhog. "From Birdtown."

"But I thought you said you were lost," said a warrior.

"Well, I mean—in a way I'm lost. But I know where I am. What I meant to say was I'm lost from my family."

"We'll take you home in our dugout canoe," said one of the warriors. "It'll save you a lot of walking. We're camping here till the sun rises, and it ought to be coming up any time now. We need daylight to navigate these rapids."

"Where are you headed?" asked Groundhog, hoping it wasn't Birdtown.

"Falltown," said a warrior. "In Creek country. We're on our way to raid it."

The first faint light of dawn was spreading over them, bringing enough light for Groundhog to see the three men. He looked at them admiringly. They were real warriors—fierce, their bodies painted red and black for war. He saw that one of the warriors, the one he had crashed into, was very tall. Another had only one ear. Groundhog liked the way they looked. He was pleased to have stumbled upon them.

With enough morning light to make their way, the three warriors headed for the riverbank. Groundhog followed and helped them push their heavy log canoe into the water.

"Hop in, little brother," said the one-eared warrior, and Groundhog clambered in.

In the misty summer dawn the warriors paddled

silently downstream. Groundhog watched the river-bank sliding by and thought about his family back home. They would be waking up now. Someone would notice he was gone. Probably Pokeberry. Kingfisher would go outside and look around for him. He would check at Jumper's house, but Jumper would pretend not to know anything. Kingfisher would come back home, shaking his head. And Groundhog's mother and Pokeberry would get worried. Grandfather would probably be the one to notice that the cold meal was missing. They would know then what had happened. Kingfisher would gulp down some breakfast and then go round up a few warriors. They would set out on his trail, stopping along the way to cut some switches. But now they would never catch him. Not with this canoe carrying him so quickly on his way.

Groundhog thought that perhaps by noon they would be at Birdtown. But noon came and they kept on going. The warriors did not talk very much, but one by one Groundhog learned their names. The tall one was Standing Bear. The one with one ear was called Squash. The third one's name was Driver and he seemed to be the leader.

"We'll soon be there," Driver told Groundhog late in the afternoon. "You'll be sleeping in your own bed tonight."

Groundhog knew he should reply by inviting them to his house for the evening. But how could he? He didn't live in Birdtown. His plan was to get out of the canoe, sneak past the town, and head downriver on foot. If he invited the warriors to his house, as any polite Cherokee would do, he would put himself in a mess he could never get out of. So he stared straight ahead and said nothing.

There was an awkward silence.

Then Standing Bear said, "Say hello to Broken Branch for me when you get home. He's an old friend of mine."

"I'll give him your greeting," murmured Groundhog.

"You *do* know Broken Branch, don't you?" said Standing Bear.

"Yes, of course," lied Groundhog.

There was another silence.

"You're not from Birdtown, are you, little brother," said Standing Bear.

"What?" Groundhog said in a fluster.

"I made up that name Broken Branch," Standing Bear said. "I don't know anybody by that name in Birdtown. I don't think you do either."

The other two warriors stopped paddling and looked at Groundhog.

"Well," said Groundhog, his face burning with the shame of being caught.

"Tell us the truth," said Driver. "Where are you from and what are you up to?"

"I'm from Frogtown," said Groundhog, blurting out the truth. "And I'm going on a raid to Rabbit-town. You can put me off here if you like. I'll go the rest of the way on foot."

"We're not putting you anywhere just yet," said Squash. "Not until we talk this over."

"We ought to take you home," said Standing Bear. "But it was way back yesterday when we passed Frog-town. It would take two days of poling upstream to get back there. Or else we'd have to leave the dugout here and walk you home. And then walk all the way back again. Either way it would use up two or three days."

"I'm not going home," said Groundhog. "If you try to take me back, I'll run away. I'm going to Rabbit-town to get my horse. The Creeks stole her, and I'm going to steal her back."

"How old are you?" asked Driver.

"Twelve, almost," said Groundhog, fudging a little. Squash rubbed his chin as he studied Groundhog. Then he said quietly to his two companions, "I've known regular warriors who were barely fourteen years old."

"He *is* tall for his age," agreed Standing Bear.

"But even so," said Driver, "he's just a boy."

"What choice do we have?" said Standing Bear. "We don't have time to take him home. And even if we did, he would probably run away again."

Groundhog nodded in agreement.

"We can either dump him out here or give him a ride to Rabbit-town," said Squash.

"If we do give him a ride, we can't make his raid for him," warned Driver. "We have a score of our own to settle with the Falltown Creeks. We can't waste our trip by raiding Rabbit-town. If we take him down there, we'll have to let him steal his horse by himself. We can't wait around."

The others nodded. They seemed to have made up their minds. Driver turned to Groundhog and spoke for the three of them.

"What you ought to do, little brother, is get out of the canoe and go back home. But we know you're not going to do that. So we're willing to help you. We pass Rabbit-town on our way to Falltown. We'll take you down there if you'd like."

"I would like that very, very much," said Groundhog. "It would make things easier for me. A whole lot easier."

"That must be quite a horse you lost," said Standing Bear.

"Her name is Midnight," said Groundhog. "She's an unusual horse."

"A fast runner?" asked Squash.

"No. Just unusual."

"She must be, for you to be going through all this," said Driver.

The warriors took up their paddles and straightened the canoe around in the current. Groundhog sat back and marveled at his good fortune. Here he was, going down the river with real warriors. Perhaps they would even lend him some war paint.

GOING ON ALONE

The three warriors and Groundhog kept silent as they traveled. They did not stop at Birdtown but went on until dusk. Then Driver pointed to the bank at a laurel tree whose leafy branches hung out low over the water. The warriors guided the dugout to it and everyone jumped out and helped push the canoe out of sight beneath the branches and tie it there. All this was done without a word. As men on the war trail, they spoke only when necessary. The silence they kept was not only to protect them from being discovered by their enemies, it was also to build up their power as warriors.

The power of warriors was something Groundhog only partly understood. It was more than strength and courage. It had to do with the spirit forces of the world. Some spirit forces were very great, like the Sun and Red Man Thunder. Others were smaller, like the spirit of a fox or a cedar tree. But each had its own power to give. If a person behaved as he should, the spirit forces would be there when he needed help—

and a man on the war trail needed all the help he could get.

After hiding their dugout, they made camp beside a small stream that flowed into the river. Though they were still in Cherokee country, they made no fire, for there was always a chance there could be Creeks about. Groundhog took his place in the camp with the others, all of them with their backs to each other, each keeping guard in a different direction. Groundhog chose a fallen log to sit on, for if a warrior sat on the bare ground, he would lose his power and the forces of the world would not help him in battle.

The four of them sat quietly for a time, watching the woods and listening to the birds. Then, just as the sun was setting, Driver took a pouch of cold meal from his belt. Because fasting was another way of building power, no one had eaten since sunset the day before.

Groundhog reached uncertainly for his pouch, watching Driver out of the corner of his eye and wondering whether he should fix his cold meal for himself or wait to see if Driver offered to do it. In a war party it was the war leader who kept charge of the food. He was the one who was closest to the spirit forces. Food from his hand had extra power.

As Groundhog watched, Driver took a little gourd dish and dipped some water from the stream. He poured into it a small bit of cold meal and stirred it with his finger and waited a moment for it to thicken into mush. Then, using two fingers together, he scooped all the mush into his mouth. When he had finished, he took cold meal from Standing Bear's pouch and made a bowl for him. Then he made one for Squash. As Squash ate, Driver looked at Groundhog.

Groundhog's finger began untying his pouch. "I have my own," he said quietly.

"Good," said Driver, and Groundhog thought he meant that he should take care of himself.

He tried not to show his disappointment at not being fed by the war leader. Taking his gourd dish from his pouch, he rose to go to the stream.

But Driver stepped over and put a silent hand on his shoulder and sat him down again. The warrior held out his other hand for Groundhog's pouch. Groundhog offered his bowl along with it, but Driver took only the cold meal. He went to the stream and prepared Groundhog's mush in the same bowl the warriors had used. Groundhog watched him stir it. Then he saw Driver open his own pouch and take out a pinch of cold meal and mix it into Groundhog's mush, giving it extra power.

Driver turned and saw Groundhog watching, and a friendly smile came crinkling through his war paint.

Groundhog slept soundly that night on branches of cedar that separated him from the earth and helped him build his power. Though he had offered to share the watch, no one wakened him until dawn.

With the first light of morning they broke camp. Standing Bear, Driver, and Groundhog pulled the dugout from the laurel, while Squash shinnied up a poplar tree, going high enough to see all around. Then he slid down again and waded into the water and climbed into the canoe without a word. They knew by his silence that there was no sign of anyone before them or behind them. No one was on the river or moving along the banks. The way was clear.

Rabbit-town was farther than Groundhog had imagined. It was late in the afternoon before the mountains of Cherokee country fell away behind them and they came into a land of rolling hills. The river here was wider and deeper.

"It's not safe anymore to show ourselves in daylight," said Driver. "We'll pull out now and hide until dark. Everyone should try to get some sleep. We'll be traveling all night."

After that they traveled only in darkness, paddling silently down the ever widening river. The first night's journey took them deep into Creek country. They passed a sleeping enemy town, gliding by it in the shadows without a sound. Groundhog could see the rooftops in the moonlight. But he felt safe with the three warriors. He was lucky to have met up with them. How else could he have ever come so far?

At dawn they hid the canoe and then found a hiding place for themselves beneath a fallen oak tree. All day they slept and watched, never making a sound. At sundown they ate, then they put into the river again. But early in the night the warriors pulled up against the bank and stopped. Before them in the bright moonlight a stream flowed out of the forest, silently emptying its waters into the river.

Standing Bear pointed up the stream. "That's the way to Rabbit-town," he whispered. "Just a little way up that stream. There's a good path beside it that will take you there."

Groundhog stared numbly in the direction he was pointing. The time had come for him to go on alone. Suddenly that did not seem like such a grand idea. He had spent four days and nights with the warriors. Leaving them would be like leaving a warm bed on a cold morning. It was not going to be easy.

Groundhog climbed slowly from the dugout.

"Thank you for bringing me down here," he said in a low voice. He was already feeling sorry for himself, abandoned. "I'm sure you will have a successful raid on Falltown. I'm sure you'll return safely to your homes."

"So will you, little brother," Squash said softly.

For a moment Groundhog stood motionless on the bank. Then with great effort he turned to walk away.

"Little brother," said Driver.

Groundhog turned back, almost hoping they would not let him go.

"If you do manage to get away with your horse," said Driver, "and if they don't bother to chase you very far, hide somewhere upriver and wait for us. We'll all go back to Cherokee country together."

Groundhog nodded gratefully.

"But listen, little brother," whispered Standing Bear. "If they come hard after you, you won't be able to come back this way. They know the paths and you don't. You would never make it. If they come hard on your heels, you'll have to go home another way, off the paths. Do you know how?"

Groundhog shook his head.

"Go north," said Standing Bear. "Use the north star to find the way. You've come southwest down this river. But go home due north. They won't think to look that way at first. When they finally figure it out, they won't bother to come after you. Especially if they have to go off the paths. It would be too much trouble for just one horse."

Groundhog remembered the warriors of his own town. "I know about things being too much trouble," he said.

"Go north until you come to Cherokee country," said Standing Bear. "Then turn east to get back over to Frogtown."

"When you turn east, you'll have to cross some high mountains," said Driver. "It will be a hard journey for you, little brother—a lot harder than it's been so far. But if they wake up during your raid and chase you, that's the safest way to go."

Groundhog stood waiting for them to say more. But they had nothing more to tell him.

"Thank you," he said at last. "Thank you for everything."

He watched the warriors push out from the bank and glide silently downstream and disappear around a bend. For a time longer he stood there, feeling alone, watching the empty river. Then he slowly turned away

and found the path beside the stream. He stopped for a moment and breathed deeply, steadying himself. He looked around at the night; the Little People of the forest entered his thoughts, and he felt less lonesome. The knee-high spirit folk were invisible unless they wanted to be seen, but you could always be sure they were around, especially at night. "Be careful of them," Grandfather had always told him, "but do not fear them. They can be as friendly as they are mischievous. Many a person has been saved from danger by the Little People."

"I am here with you," Groundhog said aloud to them as he started out along the path to Rabbit-town.

The moon was full, so bright that Groundhog could easily see his way in the forest. At first as he walked along he thought about what the warriors had said to him. He did not care for their idea of going home across the mountains. He knew about the dismal places high up in those mountains. There were giant frogs lurking there and great snakes and dark, sucking whirlpools. He would rather not go that way. He would rather come back to the river and wait for his three friends. They could all travel home together.

First he must make a good raid. He began concentrating on the spirit forces of the world, trying to build up his power while he still had time. His thoughts of the Little People reminded him of a war song he knew, one that Kingfisher had given him last winter on a cold night when his older brother had been in an unusually generous mood. It was just the song he needed now, and he began singing it to himself.

> *Hear me now! Little People! I am the same as you:*
> *Unseen, I walk the pathway of power.*
> *All right now! I am like the Wind:*
> *Unseen, I move through the treetops.*
> *Hear me now! Hummingbird! I am as swift as you:*
> *Unseen, I whiz over my enemies.*
> *All right now! My footsteps turn home in victory.*

He repeated the song four times, and when he had finished he felt that he must indeed be hard to see, his body as thin as his shadow, as Grandfather would say.

Suddenly the forest ended. Before him was a clearing so flooded with moonlight that it seemed to be lying in soft, silver daylight. In the clearing was a cornfield thick with tasseled stalks, and through the corn he could make out housetops. He stood on his tiptoes, but the corn was too tall for him to see more. He climbed a tree at the edge of the forest and, carefully peering out from a leafy branch, took a good look at Rabbit-town.

It was not big, only nine houses—he counted them. Right away he began to look for the horses. There was no herd. The horses were picketed here and there near the houses. And there were no guards. The people

here were not expecting anyone to come from Frogtown to steal back a horse.

Groundhog studied the horses, looking hard first at
one and then another, trying to pick out Midnight. He
began to worry that she might not be there. Or what if
she was there but he could not recognize her in the
dark? He looked at each one, searching for something
familiar. Then his eyes fell on a small, dark horse tied
to the door of one of the houses. There could be no
mistake. It was Midnight. He could see her clearly in
the moonlight.

Finding her was easier than he had dared to hope.
But now to get her back again. If only she could leave
the town by herself and come through the cornfield to
meet him. Perhaps if she knew he was out here. But no.
That was impossible. Besides, she was tied. He would
have to go in and free her.

Groundhog stared at the enemy town. Silent and
gray it stood in the moonlight, black shadows falling
from the eaves of the houses. He couldn't see them, but
he knew that dogs were lying in the shadows, waiting
to bark at sounds in the night. His stomach churned.
He did not feel brave.

He thought about his family—his mother and sister,
his grandfather and his brother. How sad they would
be if he didn't return. Especially his mother and Pokeberry. Even now they must be worried, and it made
him feel sorry just thinking about it. He knew they
would be remembering that other time long ago when

he himself was only a baby and his father had gone away on a raid and never returned.

Suddenly Groundhog felt a great urge to turn around and go home.

No, he thought. I need a plan, that's all. After I've made a plan I'll feel better.

From his lookout tree he studied the situation. The forest he was hiding in stood about the clearing in a great circle. In the midst of the clearing were the houses of Rabbit-town. Between some of the houses were gardens. The house where Midnight was tied was not close to any of the others. In front of it and on one side was a wide yard of bare dirt. On the other side was a garden, with a narrower yard between the garden and the house. Behind the house and the garden was a long, open space. Then a cornfield. And beyond that, the forest. The stream Groundhog had followed up from the river came out of the forest almost directly behind the house. From there the stream passed by the edge of town and, near Groundhog's lookout tree, flowed back into the forest on its way to the river.

Groundhog studied it all and worked out a plan. He would make his way through the trees along the edge of the clearing until he came to the place where the stream flowed into the cornfield from the forest. He would know then that he was behind the house where Midnight was tied, and he would turn toward the town and sneak up to it through the cornfield. The corn was tall and wonderfully thick. It would give him cover.

But when he came to the end of it, then what? There was nothing but a wide, moonlit space. Then the house with dark, shadowy eaves. He would pass around the side of the house that had the garden near it. Then he would be in the front yard with Midnight, standing with her in a pool of bright moonlight, not a shadow near. Anyone who happened to look out would see him untying her.

Groundhog was beginning to feel sick. Making a plan had not made things better. He was feeling even less brave than before.

What I need, he thought, is some time. I need to work up to it, that's all.

So he decided to carve a message for the Creeks, one like they had left at his house when they first stole Midnight. By the time he had finished, he would feel brave enough to make the attack.

Groundhog climbed down from his lookout tree and poked around until he found a nice dry hickory log. The bark was loose, but not rotten. He broke off a piece. Moving into a spot of moonlight, he took out his knife and began carving a picture message on the smooth inner side of the bark. He could not see very well, and his hands were sweaty and a little shaky. But even under the best of conditions he was not a good artist. He hoped the Creeks would be able to read his scratchings and understand that a Cherokee warrior from Frogtown had stolen Midnight while all the town slept, including the dogs.

The message tablet made Groundhog feel better. Looking at it gave him courage. He would stick it in a crack in the wall plaster near the very spot Midnight was tied.

With bravery fluttering faintly in his heart, Groundhog got to his feet. It was time to make the attack.

THE ATTACK

Without a sound, Groundhog moved from tree to tree, staying in the shadow of the forest's edge. Since he was a tiny boy he had been practicing this, and now that the time had come to be a warrior he was able to move softly and smoothly, like the rustle of a summer breeze.

He came to the place where the stream entered the clearing. He stood quietly, almost without breathing, looking toward the town. Ahead was a moonlit rooftop. Midnight, the joy of his life, was tied to that house. Groundhog took a trembling step toward the cornfield. Feeling his bravery leaving him, he fingered the message tablet stuck in his belt. No courage came flowing from it. He took another step. And another.

Don't stop now, he told himself.

Crouching low, he entered the cornfield. The corn swayed and shook, rustling loudly. He stopped and then started again, more slowly. It felt almost natural to be creeping through a cornfield. Like playing a war game with Jumper. Jumper could never find him in a

61

cornfield. It helped to think of it as a game. He began to feel calmer. He had done this so many times before.

But then the cornfield ended and Groundhog found himself staring out at the enemy town. It was so close. Blood was pounding in his head and his breath came quick and light with fear.

The patch of moonlight stretched before him, open space with no cover. Beyond it lay the house. He could see the passageway between the house and the garden. That was where he had to go. Then around to the front. Quietly, without waking any dogs.

The thought of it made him want to turn back.

Don't think, he told himself.

He stepped out into the moonlight. His mind spun, blurring. Then it stilled and sharpened, and everything seemed clear and crisp. It was like a dream with no sounds. He could barely feel his feet touch the ground. Nothing seemed real as he moved silently through the moonlight.

He reached the back of the house without making a sound. He passed through the narrow yard between the house and the garden, all going smoothly. He slipped around the corner.

There before him was Midnight, black and beautiful, dozing in the moonlight.

"It's me, girl," Groundhog whispered in his softest voice, not wanting to rush up and startle her. He reached for her rope, and she jerked her head around and looked at him. Recognizing him, she nickered. . . .

Groundhog froze in terror. The nickering rang in his ears—loud as thunder it had seemed, though actually it had been quite soft.

A little boy's head popped out of the door of the house, and Groundhog moved with a jolt. He slashed at the rope, cutting it. Grabbing his carved message from his belt, he threw it at the boy. And the next thing he knew he was running into the cover of the cornfield, gripping Midnight's rope, dragging her after him.

"Wait!" yelled the little boy. All over Rabbit-town dogs began to bark. Groundhog could hear the voices of warriors waking up and rushing out of their houses. He tried to stop and jump onto Midnight's back, but he was too weak with fear. He kept running, stumbling toward the trees.

"Wait!" the little boy shouted, chasing after him. "Wait!"

Groundhog ran faster, out of the cornfield and into the forest, pulling Midnight along. As he leaped over a fallen tree, the rope jerked out of his hand, caught in the branches. He reached for his knife, to cut it free, but his knife was gone. He had lost it.

"Will you *wait!*" demanded the little boy, rushing up out of the darkness.

Groundhog tugged at the rope. "Get out of here, kid," he growled. "Don't make me hurt you."

The little boy reached for the rope and together they wrenched it free.

63

"This way," the boy said. He grabbed the rope away from Groundhog and ran toward the stream.

"What?" said Groundhog.

"Come *on!*" the little boy yelled in a whisper. "They'll find us!"

"*Us?*" cried Groundhog, running after him. "What do you mean, us? I'm a Cherokee. I just raided you."

"Be quiet!" hissed the boy and plunged into the water, knee-deep, heading upstream away from the river.

"No, you don't," said Groundhog. "Give me my horse. I'm not going back to your town."

"I'm not either," whispered the little boy. "It's not *my* town."

"What are you talking about?" said Groundhog.

"I'm a Cherokee, too!" said the little boy. "Why do you think you can understand me? You don't speak Creek, do you?"

Groundhog was totally confused.

"I'm not a Creek," said the boy, "I'm a Cherokee. A captured Cherokee. I'm going back with you."

Groundhog saw his plan in ruins. "No, you're not," he said angrily. "I came for my horse and that's all. If I drag along a little kid, they'll catch me."

"They'll catch you anyway if you don't come with me," whispered the boy. "I know where to hide. I've planned this out a hundred times."

He had jumped onto Midnight's back and was reaching down a hand to Groundhog.

"This is crazy!" muttered Groundhog, waving the hand away. But not too far behind he heard the shouts of warriors. Without another word he jumped up behind the boy, sprawling belly first across Midnight's rump. As he pulled himself into sitting position, Midnight kept a steady pace upstream, her tracks hidden in the flowing water.

"They won't look for us this way," the boy explained softly. "It's the opposite way from Cherokee country. They'll head for the river trail instead."

The two boys rode on in silence. The town noises faded behind them until all they could hear was the soft, wet clopping of Midnight's hooves on the rocky creek bottom and the sounds of darkness—frogs and locusts and night breezes.

When the silence was deep enough, the town far enough behind, the little boy spoke softly. "They call me Duck," he said.

Groundhog made no reply. He did not want to know him. He wanted to get rid of him, send him back to the town so that the Creeks would give up the chase. He was trying to think of how to say so when Duck suddenly turned Midnight out of the large stream they were following and headed up a much smaller one that flowed into it.

"What are we doing?" said Groundhog.

"Morning's coming," said Duck. "We have to hide."

The stream was narrow, the banks close on either side. Leafy branches touched overhead, some so low that the boys had to dismount. For a long time they walked quietly upstream, picking their way slowly over the slippery rocks, not stopping until the sky began to lighten with the dawn.

"Where are we?" Groundhog asked softly as the two sat down on large rocks in the shallow water. Midnight began grazing along one of the banks.

"South of town," said Duck. "They'll be looking for us to the north. We'll stay here all day and start home after it gets dark."

Groundhog fiddled with the corner of his breech-cloth, trying to find the words he needed. "Listen," he said. "I can't take you with me. They'll chase me if I do. For one horse they wouldn't bother. But with you . . . I can't get mixed up with a little kid like you. I just came to get my horse."

"She's my horse, too," said Duck. "My Creek father gave her to me. I've only had her a few days, but already I like her. She seems to be unusual."

Groundhog smiled. "Do you really think so? What's so unusual about her?"

"I'm not sure," said the little boy. "But there's something. I've already won a race on her."

"Really?" said Groundhog, looking at Duck in surprise. He could see him more clearly now that it was getting light. He certainly looked like a Creek. But he talked like an Overhill Cherokee.

"When were you captured?" asked Groundhog.

"Two years ago," said Duck. "I was little then—only six."

"How has it been?" asked Groundhog. "Have the Creeks been nice to you?"

Duck nodded. "My Creek family adopted me and treated me like one of them. They stole me to take the place of their own little boy. Some of our people had captured him in a raid. My Creek mother was sad from that when I first came. But after she got to know me she cheered up."

"It's not very kind of you to run away from her," said Groundhog.

Duck looked pained. "This isn't *easy* for me," he said, his voice trembling. "But I've got a Cherokee mother, too, don't forget. I can still remember what she looks like. Especially at night I remember her." His chin quivered.

Groundhog did not want him crying. "What town are you from?" he asked quickly. "You talk like an Overhill."

"I am an Overhill," said the boy. "I come from Canetown."

"I don't know where that is," said Groundhog.

"Neither do I," said Duck.

"Don't worry about it," said Groundhog, suddenly realizing Duck was with him to stay. "Sometimes my grandfather goes to visit the Overhills. He probably knows where Canetown is."

The two boys sat for a while without talking. Then Groundhog asked, "Do you know the way back to the main path? We need to get to the river. That's the way I came."

"But I don't think we should go back that way," said Duck. "They'll catch us for sure."

Groundhog sighed. "Then do you know which way we have to go?"

Duck shook his head. "Don't you?" he asked hopefully.

"North," Groundhog said grimly. "We stay off all the paths and follow the north star. When we get into Cherokee country we turn east and cross some mountains—high mountains with lonely dismal places at the top. If we can make it over the mountains without being killed and eaten by monsters, we'll be home. Or I will, anyway. I don't know where Canetown is."

"We'll ask your grandfather," said Duck.

HEADING NORTH

Through the long day the boys took turns sleeping and watching, waiting for night. As dusk approached, Groundhog gave Duck his extra pair of moccasins, for Duck had come with only his breechcloth. Then, as the sun was setting, Groundhog shared his cold meal.

Duck was grateful. "I'll try not to eat much," he said, running his finger around in the gourd bowl to get out the last bit of mush.

"I think we'll have enough," said Groundhog. But to himself he was worried. He wished he had packed more cold meal.

It was almost dark when they climbed on Midnight, Groundhog in front, Duck behind.

"Which direction is Rabbit-town?" asked Groundhog as they settled into their places. "I don't want to go riding into it by mistake."

"It's that way," said Duck, pointing northeast in the evening light. "If we go straight north we won't even pass close to it."

"Let's hope we don't go too far east by mistake,"

said Groundhog and clucked Midnight forward. They rode into the forest, leaving the stream and all paths behind.

At first Groundhog found it easy to stay on course by keeping the fading light of sunset always to his left. Then the last light was gone. Groundhog went on uncertainly for a while, but with nothing to guide him, he began to worry that they were riding in circles. He pulled Midnight to a halt and craned his neck toward the night sky, searching for the north star. They were deep in a forest and overhead was nothing but leafy treetops with only here and there a star shining through. Groundhog stared up at the darkness and wondered if he would ever get home.

"Where's the north star?" asked Duck.

"How do I know?" Groundhog answered irritably. "It's up there somewhere."

Duck sat back in silence. Midnight lowered her head to graze.

"We'll have to find a clearing in the trees," said Groundhog. "Which way do you think is north? We'll guess for now and then set ourselves straight when we come to a place where we can see the stars."

"North is that way," said Duck, pointing into the darkness.

"No. I think it's this way," said Groundhog, pointing in the opposite direction.

"I don't think so," said Duck.

"It doesn't matter which way we go," said Groundhog. "When we come to a clearing, we'll find the north star and set ourselves straight."

"Let Midnight choose the way," said Duck. "Then neither of us will be wrong. Nobody can blame a horse for being wrong."

"I don't suppose it makes any difference," said Groundhog. He loosened Midnight's bridle rope. "Let's go, girl," he said, nudging her with his heels.

Midnight stood without moving.

"This is stupid," said Groundhog. "She doesn't know which way we want her to go."

"North, girl," said Duck. "Home."

Groundhog tapped her with his heels.

Midnight started walking straight ahead.

"I think we're going east," said Groundhog.

"We're going west," said Duck.

"Just so long as she's not taking us back to Rabbit-town," said Groundhog.

They rode for a time in silence. But Groundhog was uneasy, worried that they might be riding toward Rabbit-town.

"I think we should stop and wait for the moon to rise," he said. "It comes up in the east. Then we'll know where north is."

"But look," said Duck. "You can see some stars now. The trees are thinner here."

Groundhog looked up and studied the sky. "Well, look at that," he said, amazed. "The north star is ahead of us. Midnight's been carrying us north."

"What an unusual horse!" exclaimed Duck.

"Do you think she really knows which way she's going?" said Groundhog.

"I don't know," said Duck. "She's your horse. I haven't had her long enough to find out these kinds of things."

"It doesn't matter," Groundhog said happily. "We're headed home, little brother. We're on our way."

He gave Midnight an extra nudge and she trotted north through the patches of starlight until the trees closed in once more above their heads. As Midnight slowed to a walk and began picking her way slowly through the darkness, Groundhog loosened her bridle rope and let her choose the way.

They moved quietly through the night, Midnight's hooves making little noise on the soft forest floor. Groundhog listened to the summer darkness, straining to pick out any sounds that might mean pursuers from Rabbit-town. But he heard nothing to cause alarm. They seemed to be safe.

When at last the moon began to rise, Groundhog looked over through the trees and saw that it was off their right, where it should have been.

"She's doing it, little brother!" he exclaimed.

"Doing what?" asked Duck, half asleep.

"Midnight is keeping us straight. I haven't guided her at all and she's still going north."

"She really is an unusual horse," said Duck, yawning and rubbing his eyes.

Groundhog urged Midnight on. He was thinking of

his mother and sister. And of Grandfather. And of bean bread and turkey and corn on the cob.

All night they traveled, Midnight always carrying them north. They rode through forests and through scrubby meadows. They crossed trails worn deep and wide by Creek travelers, and after crossing them Groundhog always dismounted to brush away Midnight's tracks from the bare dirt. Once they passed close by an enemy town. They smelled wood smoke and heard dogs barking in the night. But they hurried by, undiscovered.

At dawn they chose a clump of young persimmon trees tangled with vines to be their hiding place for the day. As soon as there was enough light to see, Groundhog climbed a popular tree to make sure there were no Creeks nearby.

There was no sign of enemies. But to the north he saw mountains, hazy blue, standing away against the sky. They seemed to be waiting, as if they knew he was coming. He stared at them in silence, remembering stories, chilling stories. He wondered how it would be in those high places. He hoped his courage wouldn't fail him.

They took turns sleeping and watching through the day. During Groundhog's watch he explored around and found blueberries growing in a nearby clearing. Birds had gotten most of them, but he picked all that were left, and that evening he and Duck mixed them with their cold meal.

When darkness came they started out again.

75

Groundhog was no longer worrying about their course, for Midnight had not once strayed from going north. They covered a long distance that night without seeing any more signs of Creek towns.

Morning light rose again into the sky. The mountains were so close now that Groundhog did not have to climb a tree to see them. For a long time he stood facing them, watching daylight spread across them, wondering about their dismal places.

They camped that morning in a clump of young cedars near a small stream. Groundhog did not rest well. He was worried about the mountains. And his family was on his mind. The day seemed to pass very slowly.

At twilight he and Duck sat beside the stream and dangled their feet in the water as they ate their cold meal. Groundhog was unusually quiet.

"I'm not afraid of the mountains," Duck told him.

"Then you're crazy," said Groundhog.

"Why should we be afraid of the mountains?" asked Duck. "We're Cherokees. We were born in the mountains."

"We were born in the valleys," said Groundhog. "Nobody lives in the high places."

"Why not?"

"Because they are too dismal. There are too many monsters up there."

"What kinds of monsters?" asked Duck.

"Don't you know anything about mountains?" asked Groundhog.

"I was little when I was captured," Duck said. "I don't remember much about mountain monsters. But I know about Creek monsters."

"Do the Creeks have giant snakes?" asked Groundhog.

Duck nodded. "As big around as tree trunks. They live in rivers where the water is deep."

"It's the same way in the mountains," said Groundhog. "But up there the snakes don't stay in the water all the time. They hide in dark passes and wait for people to come traveling through. They jump out and wrap themselves around people and squeeze them to death. Then they drag the bodies down into their homes in the deep pools."

"And eat them?" asked Duck in a small voice.

"I guess so," said Groundhog.

Duck was silent.

They didn't talk much after that.

When the sun went down they set out on their way. They could see the mountains before them, darker than the night sky, looming closer and closer until at last they arrived in a wide valley. A low range of mountains rolled away to the west beneath the moonlight. To the east rose higher ridges.

"Are those the ones we have to cross?" asked Duck, pointing to the high mountains.

"That's right," said Groundhog, trying to sound confident. "Frogtown is somewhere on the other side."

"When do we start across?"

"I'm not sure," said Groundhog. "Let's go on a little farther. Maybe we'll see something that will show us the way."

But they saw nothing, only dark, shadowy mountains. Then, near daybreak, Midnight began to head toward them.

"She's turning east," Groundhog said uncertainly.

"She knows the way!" exclaimed Duck.

"I'm not sure about this," said Groundhog.

"Do you know a better way to go?" said Duck.

Groundhog pulled Midnight to a halt and studied the dark mountains. "You're right," he decided at last. "We don't know a better way. We'll let Midnight lead us. She's done all right so far. But first let's stop and rest a little. We'll wait until it's light before we start across."

"Is it safe to travel in the daytime?" asked Duck.

"We're out of enemy country now," Groundhog reminded him.

"That's right," said Duck. "We're almost home, aren't we?"

"If we can just get past the dismal places," said Groundhog, sliding down from Midnight's back. "I guess your mother will be surprised to see you."

"I guess she will," said Duck. He slid down and sat on the ground in a patch of moonlight. Groundhog let Midnight loose to graze and then got out the bag of cold meal, and they ate a little. Then he settled down under a tree and closed his eyes.

But sleep did not come. After a while he opened his eyes and saw Duck still sitting in the moonlight, studying his toes, digging them against the ground. He seemed worried. Groundhog felt sorry for him. Duck always acted so brave, as if nothing could bother him. Maybe it was because of the hard times he had seen. Maybe he had learned how to act that way, tough on the outside. But inside he was just a little boy.

"Listen," Groundhog said gently. "Don't worry about the dismal places."

"I'm not," Duck said miserably. He sounded like he might start crying.

"Well, in case you are worrying," said Groundhog, "I just want to tell you not to. Because . . ." he tried to think of a reason not to worry.

"I'm not worried about the dismal places," said Duck. He dug his toes into the grass. "I'm worried about my mother."

"Which one?"

"My Cherokee mother. My real one. What if she adopted another boy to take my place? Maybe she won't even be glad to see me."

"Of course she will," said Groundhog. "She's your mother."

"But what if she has another boy? What if he's eight years old, like me, and she calls him Duck?"

"I see what you mean," said Groundhog. It was something to think about.

"What will I do?" asked Duck.

Being asked for advice made Groundhog feel experienced and wise, like Grandfather. He spoke slowly, like Grandfather would. "Well, now . . . It's a little soon to be thinking about this, don't you think? If I were you, I would wait and think about it later."

"I suppose so," said Duck. He gave a deep, trembly sigh. Then he crawled over to Groundhog and curled up on the ground beside him. After a long time they both fell asleep.

THE DISMAL PLACES

When they set out again in daylight, Groundhog could see that Midnight was following an animal trail.

"I think it's an elk trail,' he said. "My grandfather says that elks have trails across the mountains."

"Maybe it will take us all the way to the other side," said Duck.

"Maybe," said Groundhog.

The mountains were so close now that he could no longer see the entire range standing tall and wide. All he could see was the slope of the first ridge and the elk trail that ran a little way ahead of them and then was lost in the trees. Midnight followed it as if she knew where she was going, and that made him feel more confident.

"I wonder if I have a grandfather," Duck said from behind. "I don't remember having one before I was captured. Is yours nice?"

"He's nice," said Groundhog. "But grouchy."

"At the same time?"

"He has rheumatism," explained Groundhog.

"Does he tell stories?" asked Duck.

"Lots of them," said Groundhog.

"About the dismal places?"

"Sometimes."

"What's up there besides snakes?" asked Duck.

"Oh, frogs and lizards and things," said Groundhog.

"Big ones?"

"Giant ones," said Groundhog.

"Do they eat people?" asked Duck.

"People, horses, birds, anything they can catch."

"Does the frog that eats the moon live up there?" asked Duck.

"He lives in the highest part. He has to be up where he can reach the moon when he jumps for it," explained Groundhog.

"I've seen him do it," said Duck. "One night I saw him take a bite out of the moon."

"Did you help scare him away?" asked Groundhog.

"We all did. Everyone in Rabbit-town. What a racket. Drums banging, whistles blowing, guns firing, people shouting. It scared the frog and he spit the moon back out again. I saw it."

Groundhog thought about the great ugly frog, the size of a house perhaps, or maybe larger. He tried to imagine how long its tongue would be. "I wouldn't like to meet up with him," he said.

"He must be big," said Duck.

"Huge," said Groundhog.

All through the morning and into the afternoon

they rode along the elk trail, up one ridge and then around, level for a way, then up again, until by late afternoon they were well into the mountains.

They stopped near a small stream to make their camp. Sliding down wearily from Midnight's back, they stretched and walked around a little and then took off their moccasins and waded in the cool stream. While there was still plenty of light they gathered cedar boughs for a bed and laid fern fronds over the cedar to make the bed soft and smooth. Then Groundhog took the bag of cold meal from his belt and they sat down beside the stream. For a little while they just rested contentedly and watched the light fade from the forest. A mockingbird sang in a laurel bush nearby. In the distance two quail called back and forth. Then a raccoon waddled into view. The boys watched it as it made its way neatly across the stream and went on, intent on some raccoon mission.

"It's nice here," said Duck as the raccoon disappeared down the slope. "It doesn't seem dismal to me."

"This isn't the high part," said Groundhog. "Wait until tomorrow."

"Maybe it won't be so bad," said Duck. He reached for the bag of cold meal that Groundhog had set on a rock between them. He shook it and then peered into it. "Do you think this stuff is going to last until we get home?"

"It has to," said Groundhog, trying to sound unconcerned.

But he could see Duck knew he was worried about it. He watched the little boy fill the gourd bowl with water and stir in just a small bit of cold meal. The mush was so thin, Duck drank it instead of scooping it out with his fingers.

"Mush soup." Duck grinned as he passed the bowl and cold meal pouch to Groundhog.

Groundhog made his mush as thin as Duck's and drank it down. "It's better than *rock* soup," he said as he wiped his mouth with his hand.

"Rock soup?"

"Plain water," said Groundhog. "The rock doesn't add very much."

He and Duck laughed. They felt good as they settled down on their bed of cedar and ferns and lazily watched the stars. The night air was cooler here than in Creek country. A blanket would have been nice. But they did not complain. As they grew sleepy, they huddled against each other for warmth. They slept soundly until morning.

Setting out again, they found the trail growing steeper. They were coming into the high mountains. When Midnight began to strain against their weight and then to stumble, the boys dismounted so she could climb more easily. Groundhog led the way now as they trudged along. Duck followed, leading Midnight. The mountains grew rockier, the trail steeper. They moved carefully along steep places where the mountainside fell away sharply beyond the edge of the path. They had come so far they could no longer see the valley country behind them. The higher they went, the more they felt alone, far away from other people. Even the trail they were following was not for human travelers.

They moved on through shadowy passes where mountains rose high on every side. In these dismal places they could sometimes hear a river rushing down a rocky gap, and whenever a view opened from the path, they would peer down the mountainside, trying to catch a glimpse of the white, swirling waters.

In midafternoon they stopped at a place where the path came close to the edge of a gorge. They could hear the sound of the river below them. Leaving Midnight to browse along the trail, the boys eased out onto a cool rock ledge. They lay down on their bellies and peered cautiously over the edge into the gorge below.

"Look at that!" gasped Groundhog.

At the bottom of the gorge they could see the river. It came tumbling down, white and foaming, over great boulders and flowed into a dark, rippling pool; there the waters calmed at first but then began to rush until, coming out of the pool, the river seemed to drop as it whipped around into a furious spin.

"Is that a whirlpool?" asked Duck.

"I think so," said Groundhog. "It must be."

"Does it scare you?" asked Duck.

"A little. If you get caught in a whirlpool, the water holds you and carries you around and around to the bottom."

"Then what?"

"The Water People live underneath it. When you get down to the very bottom of the whirlpool, they reach up and grab you."

"And eat you?"

Groundhog nodded.

Duck didn't say anything. He lay quietly, staring down at the deadly whirlpool.

"See that deep pool above it?" said Groundhog. "See how calm and dark it is?"

Duck nodded.

"A monster snake probably lives in that pool. Or maybe a giant leech."

"A leech? How big?"

"Huge. Bigger than a house. He probably stays at the bottom of the pool." Groundhog studied the dark water. "Can you see anything down there?"

"I don't know," said Duck. "It's all shadowy."

"If you fell into his pool, he would kill you. And when your body was found, all your blood would be gone and your ears and nose would be sucked off."

Duck stared down in horror. He reached up to feel his ears and nose.

Below, the calm waters of the pool suddenly swirled.

"Let's get out of here," said Groundhog. He pushed up onto his hands and knees and backed away from the edge. Then he jumped up and hurried back to the path. Duck followed close behind.

They traveled on uneasily. After the leech pool everything seemed scarier. Often they heard sounds that made them glance nervously around. They hurried past dark laurel thickets and kept a sharp eye on boulders and uprooted trees and anything else that could hide a monster snake or some other dismal creature. Toward evening they tried to find a safe place to camp. But no place seemed safe anymore.

Their supply of cold meal was almost gone. They ate only a little for their supper. When they went to sleep, they were still hungry. And they were cold. All through the night they kept waking up, hearing noises. Nearby, Midnight shifted nervously, jerking on her rope.

Dawn came at last, misty and quiet. The boys rose with an effort. Their bodies were tired and sore, their stomachs empty. Mist swirled about them as they started up the trail. All they wanted now was for their journey to be over. They hardly talked anymore.

By midmorning the fog had lifted. But the sky stayed cloudy and gray all day. Late in the afternoon a wind rose and the air grew colder.

"It's going to storm," said Duck.

Groundhog glanced nervously at the sky. "Grandfather says storms are bad in the mountains. There's a lot of lightning."

"What should we do?" asked Duck.

"We'll go up the next stream we come to," said Groundhog, "and see if it leads us to a cave."

"Not me," said Duck. "I'm not going into a cave."

"It would keep us dry," said Groundhog. "And safe."

"Safe?" said Duck. "Are you crazy? Where do giant frogs live?"

Groundhog did not answer.

"In caves," said Duck, answering for him. "They live in caves, and I'm not going into one. I'm not afraid of the rain. I'll sit right here on the trail and get wet."

"If that's what you want, it's all right with me," said Groundhog. "But Midnight and I are going to find a cave."

"You can't leave me," said Duck.

"It's up to you," said Groundhog. "You can come or not."

When they came to the next stream, Groundhog took Midnight and started up along it. At first Duck hesitated, but then he gave in and followed them. The sky was black. They could hear thunder rumbling in the distance. The wind was strong and gusty. The air smelled of rain. And night was falling.

"There!" Groundhog cried suddenly, pointing up to a black hole in the mountainside ahead of them.

They hurried toward the cave. But before they could reach it, a hard rain came beating down, and they were dripping wet by the time they stumbled into shelter. They could not see how big the cave was or how far back it went. Groundhog picked up a pebble and threw it into the darkness. It went a long way before it landed.

"Don't do that," whispered Duck. "You don't know what's back there."

"There's nothing back there," Groundhog said uncertainly.

"It's a big cave," said Duck as he sat down close to the entrance.

Groundhog stood holding Midnight's rope. There was no place to tie her and she was nervous in the storm. Lightning flashed and lit up the evening sky. Thunder shook the mountains. As the last daylight faded into night, Groundhog watched the blowing rain and tried not to think about the cave. He thought about his family, picturing each one in his mind. He had been gone so long. He wished there were some way to tell them he was all right.

"Listen!" Duck said suddenly.

It was pitch black now and the boys could barely see each other. Midnight snorted and stepped about uneasily. Groundhog tightened his hold on her rope.

"I don't hear anything," he said.

"Listen!" said Duck, getting to his knees. "Back there!"

"In the cave?" said Groundhog.

"Yes!" said Duck. "Let's leave!"

"Don't be silly," said Groundhog. Lightning flashed as he spoke. Midnight jerked her head, rolling her eyes in fright.

"Did you hear it that time?" said Duck, jumping to his feet. Thunder crashed around them.

"I didn't hear anything," said Groundhog. "Rain and thunder, that's all. You're imagining things."

90

"Midnight heard it, too," said Duck.

Groundhog was trying not to panic. "It's the storm," he said, turning and peering back into the blackness of the cave.

"It sounded like a giant frog," said Duck.

"You don't know what you're talking about."

"A giant frog," Duck repeated in a trembling voice. "He's back there. I heard him swallow."

"No, you didn't," said Groundhog. But he moved closer to the mouth of the cave. It was too dark to see anything. He strained his ears to listen.

Then he heard it. In the back of the cave. Like a grunt. A deep, quick sound. Midnight jerked her head in fright. Her rope slipped from his hands. Lightning flashed. Midnight reared and with a shrill whinny plunged out into the storm.

"The frog!" screamed Duck. "Run!"

They rushed in terror from the cave, scrambling, trying to get away. Thunder shook the darkness. On the steep mountainside Groundhog slipped and tumbled. He caught himself and jumped up running. The rain soaked him as he ran crashing through the forest.

Far from the cave he stopped and stood panting. "Are you all right?" he asked Duck.

There was no answer.

"Duck?"

No answer. Only the sound of the rain.

"Duck!" he called.

But no voice came back to him.

He turned and walked back a little way. "Duck!" he called.

He kept walking, going back the way he had come. Or was it the way? The darkness was confusing. He stopped, uncertain of his direction. But then he kept going, looking for Duck.

The rain stopped. All night long Groundhog searched for his friend, trudging up and down the steep slopes through the rain-soaked forest. He tried not to think about Midnight. When daylight came, he and Duck would find her.

But Duck himself was nowhere to be found. At last he gave up. It was no use in the dark. He had lost the cave. He had lost the elk trail. Duck was gone. Midnight was gone. Groundhog crawled beneath the low boughs of a cedar tree and curled up miserably on the cold, wet ground. Thinking about Duck and Midnight and his family back home, he waited for dawn, sometimes dozing but never really sleeping.

Things were no better in the morning. In daylight he could see how lost he was. There was no trail to be found. He had no idea where the cave was. He did not know whether to go up the mountain or down, this way or that.

He called but no one answered. What could have happened to Duck? Could he have been eaten by the frog, caught like a fly in that long, flicking tongue? Groundhog tried not to think about it.

All morning he wandered, calling to his friend. Finally he gave up. He had no idea where he was. He

was lost. The only thing left to do was to start going east. He had to find his way out of the mountains. He hoped Duck was safe someplace and could make it out on his own.

Groundhog set his course by the sun. As he walked along, he searched for a trail that would make the way easier. And every so often he called for Duck, just in case he was near.

He had only a little of the cold meal left. He was hungry and wanted to eat. But he thought of Duck and could not bring himself to eat the last of what they had. All afternoon he trudged along, stumbling through tangled laurel thickets, crawling over huge logs. But he was getting nowhere. It was too hard to go through the mountains without a trail. Everything seemed hopeless. The sun was sinking and soon it would be dark again. And he was very hungry.

He sat down on a log in despair. His stomach growled. His hand went to the pouch of cold meal on his belt. It might be the last food he would ever eat. He might never find his way out of the mountains.

"*Duck!*" he cried with all the strength he had left. Tears were starting up in his eyes.

"Groundhog!" came a faint voice.

Groundhog jumped to his feet. "*Duck!*" he called again.

"Here!" said the voice. It came from the mountain-side below.

Groundhog started running. Slipping and sliding, he made his way down the wooded slope. Sometimes he stopped and called again. Duck would answer, guiding him. Duck's voice grew louder and closer until all of a sudden there he was, grinning, sitting safely on Midnight's back.

"Midnight, too!" gasped Groundhog, rushing to them. Midnight nickered and trotted forward to meet him.

"I thought you were lost!" Groundhog cried to Duck. "I even thought the frog might have eaten you. Where did you find Midnight?"

"She found me," said Duck. "Just like she found you. I've been letting her carry me where she wanted to go all day long. She seemed to know where she was going. But I was afraid I would never see you again. I thought the frog had eaten you."

Groundhog laughed, glad to be back with these two. "Let's make camp," he said. "Tomorrow we'll try to find the trail."

"We're on the trail," said Duck, pointing down.

Groundhog looked and saw that it was true. They were standing on the elk trail.

"Leave it to Midnight," said Duck. "She knows the way."

BACK FROM THE DEAD

Going down the other side of the mountains was easier than climbing up. But Groundhog had never been so hungry. After eating the last of the cold meal, they went for a day and a night and most of another day without eating anything at all. Then on the lower slopes of the mountains they found ripe blackberries.

"Let's camp here and eat all night," said Duck, jumping down from Midnight.

"Be careful," warned Groundhog. "If you eat too much after you've been fasting, you'll get sick."

"I haven't been fasting," said Duck. "I've been starving." He plunged into the blackberry brambles and began stuffing the fruit into his mouth, smearing his hands and face with the juice.

Groundhog joined him. Nothing had ever tasted so good. But he stopped before eating his fill and pulled Duck away. "I mean it," he said. "If we keep eating, we'll get sick. Let that be all for now. We'll camp here and eat more in the morning."

They slept soundly that night and awoke rested. In the foggy dawn they stuffed themselves with blackberries, then started gaily down the slopes. Whenever the way was not too steep, Midnight trotted briskly along.

By late afternoon most of the high mountains were behind them. At the top of a low ridge they stopped and looked down on a wide river valley that spread below them on the other side.

"It looks like the Frogtown River!" cried Groundhog. Midnight needed no urging. She cantered down the last slope, carrying them into the valley. When they reached the river, Groundhog slid off her back and did a little dance to celebrate.

But Duck dismounted quietly. He sat down beneath a tree and picked up some pebbles and threw them listlessly into the river.

Groundhog went over and sat beside him. "Are you thinking about your mother?" he asked.

Duck nodded.

"It's still too early to worry about that," said Groundhog.

"I can't help it," said Duck.

"If she *has* adopted another boy," said Groundhog, "what would be so bad about it? She'll still be glad to see you."

"No, she won't," said Duck. "It would just confuse things to have me home again. I guess I would have to turn around and go back to Creek country." A tear squeezed out and trickled down his cheek.

98

"No, you wouldn't," said Groundhog. "Not after all this. If she doesn't want you, you can come live with me."

Duck gave a long sniffle and rubbed his eyes. "Thank you," he said sadly.

"I wonder how far we are from Frogtown," said Groundhog.

"Which way do we go?" asked Duck, trying to act more cheerful.

Groundhog stood up. He looked upriver. Then he looked downriver. "I don't know," he said.

"Don't worry," said Duck. "Midnight knows."

They rested a while longer, enjoying the warm summer afternoon. Midnight grazed peacefully beside the riverbank. When the boys were ready to go, they climbed onto her back and Groundhog tapped her with his heels.

"Home, girl," he said.

Midnight tossed her head, but remained standing where she was.

"Home, girl," said Duck.

She lowered her head and began grazing again.

They both dug their heels into her sides. "Home!" they commanded.

Midnight started walking straight ahead, back toward the mountains.

"Whoa!" said Groundhog. "What is this? Don't you know the way?"

Midnight turned her head and looked at them, then started grazing.

"She's not going to do it," said Duck. "What a dumb horse."

"Don't talk about my horse," Groundhog said irritably.

"What are we going to do now?" asked Duck.

"I don't know," said Groundhog.

"Haven't you ever been here before?" asked Duck.

"I haven't done much traveling," admitted Groundhog. "I'm not really a warrior yet, you know."

"You should be," said Duck.

Groundhog smiled. He almost hoped Duck's mother would not want him. It would be nice to have him around always.

"Let's sleep here tonight," said Groundhog. "Then in the morning we'll figure out something. Maybe if we go back up on that last ridge where I can see all around, I'll recognize the way."

"That's fine with me," said Duck. "We can stay here as long as you want. I'm not in any hurry to get home."

"Your mother is going to be glad to see you," Groundhog said as they dismounted.

"I hope so," Duck said quietly.

That night they stayed up late, talking about things, then slept past dawn and into the morning. It was the sound of horses coming up the river trail that awakened them.

Duck sat up.

Groundhog jumped to his feet. "Come on!" he said and ran to grab Midnight's rope. Then he and Duck scrambled into a thicket, pulling Midnight after them.

"If they're Cherokees, we can ask them the way home," said Duck.

"Hush!" said Groundhog. "They could be Creeks. A raiding party."

The boys waited in silence. Then the riders came in view—three warriors leading a string of horses. One of the warriors had a missing ear.

"Friends!" cried Groundhog, leaping out of the bushes.

The warriors wheeled their horses toward him, reaching for their weapons.

"It's me!" cried Groundhog, waving his arms in greeting.

They burst into smiles. "Little brother!" cried Squash. "You made it after all!"

The three jumped from their horses and crowded around him.

"I see your raid was successful," said Groundhog.

"How about you, little brother?" said Standing Bear. "Did you get your horse?"

Groundhog looked back at the thicket. "Come on out," he said to Duck. "These are friends of mine."

Duck came out cautiously, leading Midnight.

"Who's that?" asked Driver. "He looks like a Creek."

"He's a Cherokee," said Groundhog. "The Creeks captured him a couple of years ago. He came back with me."

Squash stepped toward Duck and peered closely at him. "Are you an Overhill?" he asked.

Duck nodded.

"Where from?"

"Canetown," said Duck.

"I *thought* so!" cried Squash. He looked at his companions and laughed. "This boy's supposed to be dead!" He looked back at Duck. "You're Duck, aren't you? Your mother thought you'd been killed."

"I wasn't killed," said Duck. "I was stolen. Do you know my mother?"

"I used to live in Canetown," said Squash. "I lived there until last year."

"Then you know my mother?" said Duck.

"Your mother, your father, your uncles, your grandmother. I know them all."

"Tell me about my mother," said Duck.

"Your mother? She's fine."

"Fine?"

"Well, she was awfully upset when you were killed —I mean, captured. We thought she would never get over it. Then she adopted another boy."

"See there!" Duck said to Groundhog, trying not to cry. "What did I tell you?"

"But she didn't keep him very long," said Squash.

"She didn't?" said Duck.

"She said he was a nice boy, but he wasn't Duck. And she felt sorry for his mother. He had been taken from Creek country. So she sent him back home again with some travelers who were passing through Canetown."

Duck smiled happily. "Then she doesn't have anybody else."

"Only the new baby."

Duck's smile vanished. "Oh," he said quietly.

"What's wrong with that?" said Groundhog. "It would be fine to have a little brother. I wouldn't mind having one myself."

"It's a girl," said Squash.

"Sisters are fine, too," said Groundhog. "It all sounds very nice to me."

"Then you think my mother will be glad to see me?" said Duck.

"Glad?" said Squash. "She'll be the happiest mother around. I'm going to take you home myself, just to get in on the celebration. There'll probably be a feast. And dancing."

Duck beamed.

"Duck's not the only one coming back from the dead," said Standing Bear. "Our young warrior brother here is going to surprise some folks when he comes riding in."

"They don't think I'm dead," said Groundhog.

"Some of them do," said Standing Bear. "We just left Frogtown this morning. It's your grandfather who's kept them from having your funeral. The rest of the town thinks you're dead."

"You were there this morning? I must be almost home!" said Groundhog.

"Don't you know where you are?" asked Driver, laughing.

"Well," said Groundhog, trying not to sound lost, "I more or less know where I am."

"You'll be home by noon, little brother," said Driver. "Just follow this trail down the river. We'll take Duck with us."

Groundhog and Duck looked at each other. After all they had been through, it hardly seemed right that they should have to split up like this.

The warriors sympathized. "Next time we come down this way, we'll bring Duck to visit you," said Standing Bear.

"And you can come up with your grandfather," said Duck.

Groundhog nodded and they both tried to smile.

"Take good care of Midnight," said Duck. "She was my horse for a while, you know."

"Do you need a horse?" Driver said to Duck. He motioned to the string of horses they were leading. "Pick one."

"Are those Creek horses?" asked Groundhog.

"They used to be," said Standing Bear and laughed.

"Take any one you want, little brother," Squash said to Duck. "A present from us."

Duck smiled his thanks. He went over to the horses and walked among them, carefully checking the legs and hooves of each one.

"Kind of particular, aren't you," teased Standing Bear. "I suppose you'd like to look at their teeth."

"Yes, please," said Duck. "Would someone help me? I can't reach them when they toss their heads."

"He's very practical," said Groundhog as Squash went over to help.

Groundhog stood back with the other two warriors and watched. He found himself studying Squash's missing ear. From the beginning he had wondered about that ear. "Has your friend ever been in a leech pool?" he asked quietly.

"Do you mean how did he lose his ear?" asked Standing Bear.

"Yes," said Groundhog. "I've been wondering."

The two warriors looked at each other and laughed.

"His wife bit it off," Driver confided.

"His *wife!*"

"She used to be his wife." Standing Bear chuckled. "They aren't married anymore."

"I guess not," said Groundhog, laughing with them. He liked these warriors. He liked the way they treated him like one of them.

Duck picked out a brown mare with a black mane and tail and led her from the herd. "The best in the herd," he said. "Want to race?"

"No!" said Groundhog.

"Why not?" said Standing Bear. "I thought you told us your horse is unusual."

"She is," said Groundhog. "But there's nothing unusual about winning a race. Lots of horses win races."

"What *is* so unusual about your horse?" asked Squash.

"She brought us back from Creek country," said Groundhog. "She was the only one who knew the way."

"It's true," said Duck. "Except when we got here to the river. Then she didn't know which way to go."

"The hard part was over by then," said Groundhog. "Maybe she thought she had done enough."

"That's right," said Duck. "She was letting us take over."

The three warriors glanced doubtfully at each other. But Groundhog did not care what they thought. He was looking at the downriver trail. Home was just a short ride away.

He turned back to the three warriors. "Did you tell them in Frogtown that you had seen me?"

"We told them how we met up with you and gave you a ride down the river. We told them that the last time we saw you, you were heading off all by yourself to make a raid on Rabbit-town."

Duck looked proudly at Groundhog.

"That was a long time ago," said Groundhog.

"Ten days," said Squash. "And even longer since you left home. Your brother and some warriors went looking for you the morning they discovered you were gone. They went all the way to Rabbit-town. But they went on foot, not knowing you had gotten a ride, and they didn't get there until after you had made your raid and were gone. They weren't sure what had happened. They saw parties of Creek warriors coming back to Rabbit-town after giving up a search of some kind. They saw that Midnight was not in the town and figured you had stolen her and were headed home. So

they turned back. But when they got home to Frogtown, you weren't there. They didn't know you were
coming home the long way. No one knew what to
think. Some thought you'd been killed. They were
ready to give you a funeral. Some thought you'd been
captured. They wanted to go back down and try to
free you. Others thought you had gotten lost and had
wandered in circles until you died. They wanted to
give you a funeral, too. But your grandfather said you
were on your way home and that everybody should
just wait."

"How did he know that?" asked Groundhog.

"He said you were too young for the Creeks to kill
you. And if they captured you, they wouldn't want to
keep you. And he knew you had taken so much cold
meal with you that you'd find your way home before
you starved to death."

"And he also said that you have a strong heart,"
added Driver. "He grumped when he said it, but I
think he meant it as a compliment."

Groundhog felt proud that Grandfather had said
that about him. Suddenly he wanted very much to be
home. He turned and jumped onto Midnight's back.

"We will see you again," said Driver. "Each of us
will meet again."

Groundhog nodded, warriorlike.

Duck grinned and waved.

Groundhog turned Midnight and started down the
trail, then stopped and turned and came trotting back.

"We meet again," said Squash.

Groundhog laughed. "I've been wondering," he said. "Could I borrow some war paint?"

"Hop down off that horse, little brother," Squash said. "We'll paint you ourselves."

They covered Groundhog with paint—his arms, his chest, his back, his legs, his face. He was divided down the middle, one side of him red, one side black. Around each eye they painted a white circle.

"It looks wonderful," Duck said admiringly. "Are you going to give a victory whoop when you ride into town?"

"I am thinking about it," said Groundhog.

He climbed up on Midnight again, thanking the warriors. Then he rode away, following the trail toward home.

Just as he came in sight of Frogtown, Groundhog pulled Midnight to a halt. Now that he was so close, he was suddenly nervous. He took a deep breath to calm himself. In his mind he went over exactly what he was supposed to do.

When he was ready, he urged Midnight to a gallop, and down one rise and up another they went, until the houses of Frogtown stood before them. Groundhog screamed out the victory cry. As Midnight galloped toward the town, he kept up the cry, filling the air with whoops and yells.

People dropped what they were doing and came running. Groundhog slowed Midnight to a canter as he approached the gathering crowd. At first no one

Victor Kalin

recognized him. Then his friend Jumper pushed forward.

"That's Groundhog's horse!" he cried.

"That's my grandson!" boomed a voice. Grandfather came striding out to meet him, smiling proudly.

"I told them you would find your way home," he said.

"It was Midnight," said Groundhog. "She was the one who knew the way."

Grandfather reached up and took the bridle rope and began leading his grandson through the town in a true warrior's homecoming. As he walked, he sang:

"Look here at this warrior!
Strong of heart!
Alone he meets the enemy!
In triumph he returns!

"Look here at this horse!
This unusual horse!
This horse knows things!
She knows her way around!"

Singing loudly, Grandfather led them four times around the town. Groundhog saw Pokeberry watching, all excited. And there was his mother, crying happily. Jumper was leaping and waving. Kingfisher was standing with his arms folded, grinning proudly and shaking his head. Groundhog was glad that none of them spoiled the ceremony by running up to hug him like a child.

The procession stopped in front of Groundhog's house. As he slid down from Midnight, everyone crowded around. He turned in a circle, beaming, trying to speak to everybody. Then Jumper appeared at his elbow and offered to take Midnight to the pasture, and he heard his mother telling everyone to let him rest now, that they could all talk to him that evening at the victory dance.

"Victory dance?" he said as she steered him through the door of their house.

"That's going too far," grumbled Grandfather, leading the rest of the family in after them.

"But he did have a victory," said Kingfisher. "He stole a horse."

"And rescued a captive," added Groundhog.

Everyone looked at him.

"Well, sort of," he said. "It wasn't that I meant to. It all kind of happened like an accident. Everything."

"All an accident," muttered Grandfather. "I'm not surprised." He was his old self again as he rubbed at his rheumatism and sat down stiffly on a bed.

"Tell us all about it," said Kingfisher.

"After he eats," said Pokeberry.

He watched hungrily as she spooned up a bowl of meat and beans and handed it to him.

"Don't eat too much," warned Kingfisher. "And take it slowly."

"You're thin," his mother worried as he scooped the food into his mouth.

"Oh, he's always been skinny," said Grandfather.

111

Groundhog was beginning to feel dizzy from all the fuss. The next thing he knew Kingfisher was taking away his empty bowl and saying, "Tell us everything that happened." They were all looking at him, waiting.

Groundhog looked back at them blankly. The entire adventure seemed too far away to talk about, like a dream a long time ago.

"How did you get away from here that night?" asked Pokeberry. "None of us heard you."

"He's already told us," said Grandfather. "It was an accident, everything was an accident."

"Not that part," said Groundhog. "I had it all planned out for how I would leave. It took a lot of sneaking. Once I got out of the house, I had to get into the cornfield without the guards' seeing me. I waited in the shadows for a long time until a cloud finally covered up the moon. . . ."

Groundhog settled into his story, and not even Grandfather interrupted as he told them about meeting the warriors and going down the river, about the attack, about Duck and the giant frog and everything, all the way to the end.

When he had finished, Kingfisher said, "You'll have to put it all into a dance for tonight."

"A dance?"

"You can't have a victory celebration without acting out the victory for everyone to see."

Groundhog was horrified. "Act it out? How can I? I didn't do anything on my own except leave town. If it hadn't been for the three warriors I never would have gotten to Rabbit-town. When I made the raid, I messed it up. If it hadn't been for Duck, I'd have been caught. If it hadn't been for Midnight, I would never have gotten home. There's nothing for me to dance about."

"Nothing?" said Grandfather, getting to his feet. "There's sneaking through the woods around Rabbit-town." The old man bent over and lifted one foot, put it down slowly on tiptoe, lifted the other, and looking carefully about, darted in a tiptoe dance from one imaginary tree to another.

Groundhog smiled.

"There's creeping through the cornfield for the attack," said Grandfather and crouched low, parting the imaginary corn before him. "And dashing through the moonlight to the front of that Creek house." The old man pranced across the room, ducking and sneaking. "Then Midnight sees you," said Grandfather, and he became the horse, standing still, hanging his head, sleeping in the moonlight—then jerking up suddenly and looking around and nickering at Groundhog.

They all laughed, Groundhog hardest of all.

Grandfather went on, dancing it all out to the very end. Then he stopped and rubbed his back and scowled. "This rheumatism," he said and sat down slowly.

"That was good," said Groundhog. He was excited now about the dance. "I'll need someone to play Duck's part," he said.

"Maybe Jumper will do it," said Kingfisher.

"And you can be one of the three warriors," Groundhog told him.

"I'll go out and find two others," said Kingfisher. "We'll come back here and start practicing."

"And ruin my afternoon nap," grumbled Grandfather. "All for a lot of nonsense."

Nonsense? Groundhog felt a pain. Why must Grandfather always be so mean?

But then he saw his mother laughing. "You can be the giant frog," she teased the old man.

Grandfather looked at Groundhog, his eyes sparkling. *"Grump!"* he said in a deep voice and flicked out his tongue at a fly.

ABOUT THE AUTHOR

JOYCE ROCKWOOD has spent most of her life in Georgia. She studied anthropology at the University of Georgia, where her husband, Charles Hudson, is Professor of Anthropology. Together they have immersed themselves in researching the culture and history of the Indians of the South. Her previous novels about Cherokees, *Long Man's Song* and *To Spoil the Sun*, received wide critical acclaim. *To Spoil the Sun* was named an ALA Notable Book of 1976 and an International Reading Association honor book.